MEET THE AUTHOR - CATHERINE MACPHAIL

What is your favourite animal?
Elephant
What is your favourite boy's name?
David
What is your favourite girl's name?
Sarah
What is your favourite food?
Mussels
What is your favourite music?
Mary Black
What is your favourite hobby?
Writing

MEET THE ILLUSTRATOR - KAREN DONNELLY

What is your favourite animal?
Woodlice!
What is your favourite boy's name?
Laurie
What is your favourite girl's name?
Jean
What is your favourite food?
Sausages and runny eggs
What is your favourite music?
Beck
What is your favourite hobby?
Drawing and printmaking

To Morag and Jimmy
for always being there

Contents

Chapter 1
Picking on Percy

Percy was asleep in the maths lesson again. Mrs Hume, the teacher, was a bit deaf so she didn't hear him snoring.

I looked across at my pal, Sammy Boy, and winked at him. Then I looked at Percy. Sammy Boy smiled. Percy asleep again? This was too good to miss.

"Go for it, Shawn," Sam said softly.

We lifted the lids of our desks and let them drop with a bang.

Percy let out a yell. Mrs Hume heard that all right. She jumped three feet in the air and let out a yell of her own.

"Percy Brown! What do you think you are playing at?" she yelled.

Percy gulped. "Please, Miss, it wasn't me," he said.

I started to laugh. Percy had an awful voice like a wailing cat. If I was Percy I'd keep my mouth shut.

"It wasn't him, Miss," I wailed, in Percy's awful voice.

Sammy Boy began to laugh. "The lid of my desk slipped out of my hand. That's what woke Percy up," I went on.

Mrs Hume almost had a fit. "Woke him up? Were you asleep again, Percy?"

Percy gave me an angry look. I don't know why. What had I done? I'd told her it was me who had slammed the desk, hadn't I?

He had the cheek to come up to me in the playground later. "One day you're going to be sorry you picked on me, Shawn," he wailed.

"One day you're going to be sorry you picked on me, Shawn," I wailed back at him. "I don't think!" I added in my own voice.

Picking on Percy was such a laugh. As I said to Sammy Boy, "Picking on Percy's the best fun you can have without a football."

Percy's the smallest boy in the class. He's always got mess on his blazer. You can tell what he had for his breakfast. Today it was porridge.

His trainers are cheap, plastic ones. We all laugh at them. The rest of us have proper ones. I'd die if I had to wear Percy's trainers.

Another bad thing is that Percy hates football! He says he likes reading better.

How could anyone with any sense like reading better than football?

The bell rang and Percy went off, trying to look cool. But, he tripped over the laces of his cheap trainers and fell flat on his face. I was still laughing as I went into my next class.

That was when I bumped into Laura. Now, Laura fancies me. You see, I'm the best football player in the school. A lot of the girls fancy me. Except Rebecca. She's the one I like best. And the truth is, Laura, who does fancy me, is ugly. In fact, she's the ugliest girl in the school.

"Hello, Shawn." Laura smiled at me.

"Goodbye, Laura," I said.

"She fancies you," Sammy Boy told me with a laugh.

I didn't think that was at all funny.

"I wish SHE fancied me," I said, pointing to Rebecca. She only looked at me when she wanted to say something bad about me. Oh, well, that was her loss. She was a snob. And I hate snobs.

Chapter 2
Magic Mo

That day, I popped into the amusement arcade on the way home from school. It was fate. I didn't go there often. So why did I go that day? I just don't know.

And who do you think I saw? Percy. He was looking at a machine right at the back. A machine I'd never seen before. I came up behind him and made him jump.

"So what does this machine do?" I asked, and pushed in front of him.

"It's called Magic Mo," wailed Percy in that awful voice.

The kind face of Magic Mo was looking at me. He had a long beard. There were lights all around his head and his eyes flashed. It was hard to look away from those eyes.

"Magic Mo can turn you into the person you most want to be," Percy said. "I'm going to put my money in and see what happens."

I began to laugh. "And who do you most want to be, Percy? David Beckham? Bart Simpson? Or maybe ... you'd like to be me?"

Percy pushed the money into the slot. "I can think of nothing more awful!" he snapped.

Percy had never been so cheeky with me before.

"And I can't think of anything worse than being you, Percy!" I told him.

Just then the machine went bananas. Lights began to flash and pop all around Magic Mo's head. The machine moaned and yelled. Magic Mo looked alive. His smile seemed to grow wider. He seemed to laugh.

My hair stood on end.

Then, it was all over. The noise of the machine was just a hum again and the light went out of Magic Mo's eyes.

"Percy! What was all that about?"

But when I looked round for Percy, he had gone. And a good thing for him too, because I was about to get back at him for all that cheek. So I went home.

That was when the bad dream began.

****

I banged on my front door. Mum opened it but not very wide.

"Hi, Mum," I said, and I tried to go in. She held out her hand to stop me.

"Mum?" she asked. "Why are you calling me *Mum*?"

I laughed. "Well, I'm your son, aren't I?" But my voice was all funny. "I'm your son, Shawn," I told her. I was her only child!

I smiled at her but she didn't smile back. Your own mum should know who you are. But she looked puzzled.

"I'm home!" I told her.

"But who are you?" said my mum. "My Shawn's been home for ten minutes."

And she was right. Just then someone who looked just like me came out of the living room and stood behind her.

But it wasn't me, because I was out here in the street.

"I know who you are!" my mum said. "You're Percy Brown. What are you doing here?"

"Did you say ... Percy Brown?" This was getting very bad.

"You go off home, Percy!" said my mum and slammed the door in my face.

Then I had an awful shock. I could see myself in the glass panel of the door. And it wasn't me at all but PERCY!

So that was why my mum had shut me out. I had Percy's messy blazer, cheap, plastic trainers – the lot.

I began to shake. Just at that moment, my front door opened again and there was the person who looked just like me.

"I'm still me, Percy, inside!" the person said. "I just look like you. It's a real mix-up."

"I know," I said. "I don't understand either but even if I'm living in your body, I'm still Shawn inside."

Percy was shaking. "I went home and my mum shut me out too. She thought I was you. In fact, she was very cross with me. She said I bullied you."

"I don't bully you. I only pick on you a bit," I said.

"Bully me, pick on me, it's the same thing," he said.

"I don't want to be you," I told Percy.

"And I don't want to be you, Shawn," he said. "Your mother keeps singing opera to me out of tune."

My mum called from the kitchen. "Shawn, come on. I've got your pizza for you."

Pizza. My best meal! But she wasn't talking to me. I was Percy now. I couldn't go in.

"I'd better go," said the real Percy softly. And then he added, "I hate to tell you, but it's egg and chips night at my house."

The door shut in my face. I could see my face again in the glass panel of the door.

I still looked like Percy. PERCY!

This had to be a bad, bad dream.

Chapter 3
Baby from Hell

I walked away. I didn't know where I was going and I didn't care. What was I going to do? I was really scared. What was going on? Who could I tell? Who would believe me?

I heard a shout behind me. "Percy! Percy Brown!" I went on walking.

Then I was grabbed from behind.

"You're late for your paper round. Again!" It was Mr Harkins, from the paper shop. He dragged me into the shop.

Paper round? Percy had a paper round?

Mr Harkins hung a big bag full of evening papers round my neck. "If you're late one more time I'll take money off your wages."

I was going to tell him where he could stick his papers, but I didn't think he was in any mood to listen.

"But where do I deliver them?" I asked as he was pushing me out of the shop.

"Forgotten, have you?" He pointed a finger at the three tower blocks at the top of the hill. "Up there!" he snapped.

****

None of the lifts worked in the tower blocks. By the time I'd walked up all those stairs, my legs felt like jelly. I was so hungry that I was even looking forward to egg and chips at Percy's house.

I went home to Percy's. And do you know where Percy lived? Yes. On the tenth floor of one of those tower blocks! We teased him about it at school.

I banged on Percy's door. It was opened by Percy's mum, Mrs Brown. "Hello, dear, you're late. I've kept your egg and chips hot in the oven for you."

In her arms was the Baby from Hell. He had dried-up food all over him. When he saw me he gave a yell and flung himself at me like a rocket.

"He just loves you, Percy," said Mrs Brown. "Don't you, Archie?"

Archie! She had called one of her sons Percy and the other Archie. Yuck!

Archie's messy fingers were all over my face and hair. It was disgusting.

I sat at the table with Archie on my lap while Mrs Brown fetched my dinner from the kitchen. I looked at the plate of dried-up egg and greasy chips. It must have been in the oven for a long, long time.

"Come to Mummy, Archie," she said, taking the baby from me. "Let Percy enjoy his tea."

Enjoy? Was she mad? I looked at the plate for a long time. All I could think of was my mum's pizza. I could just see the real Percy, sitting in front of my TV, stuffed with my pizza.

Then I felt two pairs of eyes staring at me. I blinked. Two little girls were standing in front of me. They looked so alike they must be twins. Yes, that was it. Percy's twin sisters.

Morag and Agnes. Their names were on
the beads they were both wearing round
their necks. Morag and Agnes! That was
almost as bad as Percy and Archie.

"Tell us a story!" said Morag.

"You're just so good at telling stories, Percy," Agnes added.

Me? Tell a story? I couldn't tell a story to save my life. I looked over at Mrs Brown for help.

"Just don't make it too scary, Percy," Mrs Brown said.

So I told them a story about the wicked wizard from Wales. Well, I don't know where that story came from. There must still have been a bit of Percy deep down inside me. It was a great story. Even I was longing to know the end.

That was great, I thought as soon as I'd finished.

"You always tell great stories, Percy," said Morag.

"You're the best big brother in the world."

And Agnes threw herself at me and gave me a big, wet kiss. Yuck! Poor Percy. Did he have to put up with this every night? I was beginning to feel sorry for him.

I fell into Percy's bed that night. I was worn out and a bit scared too.

How had I got into this mess? It had to be just a bad dream and I would wake up tomorrow, safe and sound, in my own bed.

Chapter 4
I'm not Percy!

"Wake up, Percy. It's time to get up."

It was still dark. Percy's dad was shaking me.

"Time to get up? I've only just got to bed."

I looked at the clock. It was six o'clock.

"You're going to be late for your paper round."

"Another paper round? But it's the middle of the night! Have I gone mad?"

Mr Brown nodded. "Well, I think you're mad, Percy," he said. "And you're only doing it to get those smart trainers. There's nothing wrong with the ones you've got."

Was this true? Was Percy working like a slave to save up for trainers like mine?

I dragged myself out of bed and went off to the paper shop.

Mr Harkins was waiting for me at the door. He grabbed hold of me. "Mrs Jones rang," he said, shaking me as if I was a rag doll. "You let the dog eat her evening paper."

"It was either that or the dog was going to eat *me*," I told him.

Mr Harkins shook his head. "Next time you'd better let it eat you, or there will be no more paper rounds for you."

It was just the same. None of the lifts in the tower blocks were working. By the time I got to school, my legs were like jelly again. Now I knew why Percy hated P.E. He was worn out.

I fell asleep in maths.

And do you know what? My pal, Sammy Boy, woke me up with the old 'slam down the desk' trick. Mrs Hume went crazy! She told me if I fell asleep again in her class she would send me to the Head.

In the playground, I tried to tell Sammy Boy what it was all about. "Don't you *understand*? I'm not really Percy Brown!"

But I spoke with Percy's awful voice. Sammy Boy began to copy me. He was sure I was Percy. Who else could I be?

"Who do you think you are, then?" he wailed. And Sammy Boy began to laugh. He shouted across the playground, "Hey, Shawn, come on over here and help me teach this wimp a lesson."

He thought it was me standing on the other side of the playground, leaning against the wall. But it was Percy trapped inside my body.

Percy was lucky. He had it made. He had a mum who could cook. And I was very good-looking as well, even if my nose was a bit big.

All this time, Sammy Boy was still shaking me. This was going too far.

I twisted free. "You're not going to teach me a lesson," I said. "You should be ashamed of yourself. I'm a lot smaller than you are."

Sammy Boy was shocked. Percy had never talked back to him before.

"So what are you going to do about it, you little wimp?" he said. "Hit me on the jaw or kick me on the shins? You just try it."

"I'm getting angry now, Sammy Boy," I said.

Sammy Boy thought this was very funny. "I'm getting angry now, Sammy Boy," he wailed in Percy's awful voice.

That did it! I lifted my foot and kicked him as hard as I could on the shins.

While he was jumping about in agony, I yelled, "I can't help the way I talk. I've got something wrong with my nose."

I remembered too late how big Sammy Boy was. As his fist came up to my face, I knew that in a few seconds I really would have something wrong with my nose.

Chapter 5
Nightmare Time

Next thing I knew, I had blood gushing from my nose. The real Percy was standing over me.

"I want to be myself again. I don't like being Percy," I said.

"Well, you did kick him on the shins first." This was Percy, the real Percy speaking. Only he looked like me. And he

was sticking up for Sammy Boy! It couldn't
be true.

"Hey, it's me you've got to stick up for!"
I told him, as he was helping me up. "After
all, we're both in this mix-up together."

Sammy Boy had gone off somewhere.

Just then, the real Percy was pushed aside. There, standing next to me, was the lovely Rebecca.

"You buzz off, Shawn," she snapped at Percy. "You're just a bully. Come on, Percy," she said to me, "I'll take you to the nurse."

I thought it was a bit unfair that she snapped at Percy, even though she did think he was me. After all, it was Sammy Boy and not Percy who had punched me.

"Shawn was only helping me up," I told her.

"You're too nice, Percy," she said to me as she took me off to the nurse.

Rebecca had never been nice to me before. This was great, even if she thought I was Percy.

The Head was waiting for me at the nurse's office. "I'm told you hit Sam," he said.

Now I knew where Sammy Boy had gone. "He punched me, sir." I pointed to my nose which was still bleeding.

"Only after you kicked him, I'm told," said the Head.

I had to admit that. "He's always picking on me, sir," I told the Head.

"I know he's given you a hard time, Percy. But you must never use force to defend yourself."

At that moment, all I wanted was to get to the nurse. I sniffed and dripped more blood, but the Head did not seem to see.

"Sam and Shawn will *both* be punished for giving you a hard time."

Both! Poor old Shawn – Percy, I mean!
He was going to be punished and he hadn't
done a thing.

"But I have to say," the Head went on,
"that Shawn seems to be a changed boy.
He has been very helpful today at school.
And do you know what? He's just joined the
school choir. He has a lovely voice."

I began to choke. *Me*, Shawn, sing in the
school choir! What was Percy trying to do
to my image? Well, two could play at that
game.

"I'll try to be a changed boy as well, sir,"
I said, in Percy's awful voice. "Put me down
for the football team."

I'd like to see Percy's face when he hears
about that!

Chapter 6
Worst Day of My Life

That day was as bad a day as it could be. I'd never understood how much Percy got picked on. Just because he was small. Just because he was skinny. Just because there was dried food all down his blazer. And just because he had that awful voice. And I kept tripping over his blinking shoelaces!

I thought hard as I walked home. Home. Where was home? I had to go back to Percy's, and the Baby from Hell. I was thinking so hard, I walked right into the arms of Mr Harkins.

He lifted me by the ears and dragged me into his shop. This was too much.

"Put me down!" I yelled.

"You're a no-good little wimp of a boy!" Mr Harkins yelled back at me. "And if you don't do better, you're fired."

"You don't have to fire me," I shouted. "I quit. I don't need smart trainers that much."

He looked amazed. His false teeth nearly fell out with the shock of it.

I began to make a quick exit from the shop.

"Let me tell you this, boy," Mr Harkins yelled after me. "You'll never get a job delivering papers in this town again."

"Good!" I yelled back at him.

****

When I told Percy's mother she was thrilled.

"I'm so glad. I never wanted you to work for that awful man."

Baby Archie was so happy he was sick all over me. And the story I told Morag and Agnes that night was the best ever. Now all I had to do was to tell Percy.

He should have been pleased. But he went bananas. He stamped about the playground as if he'd gone mad.

"I had almost saved up the money to get those trainers. And you've messed up everything," shouted the real Percy.

"You don't need them. I promise that I'll never wear mine again," I told him.

"I know you won't, pal," Percy laughed. "You see, your mum took me shopping yesterday and I made her buy me the plastic kind. I said everyone was wearing them in school now."

I was shocked. What a rotten thing to do.

"You're going to be sorry for that!" I yelled at him.

I could see people in the playground begin to laugh at us. That was the last straw. I jumped on him and down we went in a heap.

"I can't hit you," he kept on saying. "You're a lot smaller than me."

"Don't let that stop you," I said. And I hit him right between the eyes.

I would have hit him again, but just then I was pulled off Percy by the Head himself.

Chapter 7
Nobody Loves Shawn

"Percy, Percy, Percy! What do you think you're doing?"

I was sitting in the Head's office and he was telling me off.

"You're not yourself," he said.

I know I'm not myself, I wanted to shout at him. But he'd never understand.

"And don't blame Shawn," he said. "There were people nearby who have told me that he refused to hit you back because you're smaller than he is."

Great! I felt like hitting the real Percy all over again.

The Head gave me a warning letter to take home to Mrs Brown. But I didn't go back to Percy's house after school. I went back to my own house. I'd had enough of this, enough of being Percy. I wanted to be myself again.

I could hear my mum singing as I walked up the street. Then another voice joined hers, singing with her.

It was Shawn's voice. My voice. But it was Percy singing.

I went to the front window and looked inside. There they were, my mum and Percy singing away together. I'd never seen her look so happy.

Why would she want to have me back? She liked the new Shawn better. Everybody did. Percy had been inside my body for three days and he'd turned me into a really nice boy.

And what had I done for Percy? I'd lost him his job. He was going to be punished at school. I was going back to his house with a warning letter from the Head. I'd never felt so awful in my life.

In the end, I didn't bang on the door. I went back to Percy's house. On the way I met Mrs Jones and her dog. He was hungry again so I gave him the Head's letter. He ate it in one gulp.

When I walked in, the Baby from Hell threw himself at me, yelling with joy.

"That baby just loves you," Percy's mum said.

"You're the best big brother in the world," Morag and Agnes said together.

But it was Percy they loved.

Not me.

Nobody loved Shawn.

****

I stood in the playground the next day on my own. I still felt bad.

"I want to go back to being myself," I heard someone say.

I looked up. The real Percy was standing there, looking as bad as I felt.

"Why should you want to be you again?" I asked him. "You've got it made. My mum spoils her only son and she's a good cook

even if she's singing all the time. It's a pretty good life."

"I miss my family," Percy said. "I miss the baby."

"I wish he'd miss me sometimes," I said. "Like this morning when he threw his porridge at me."

Then we both started to laugh.

People looked at us, puzzled. Rebecca was all ready to run over and rescue Percy from wicked Shawn.

I saw Sammy Boy too, watching us. He looked puzzled too. I knew then that Sammy Boy would never be a pal again. He wasn't my sort.

"I'll never laugh at the mess on your blazer again," I told Percy. "Now I know what a good shot your baby is."

Percy laughed. "He always gets you just when you're going out the door."

We were both silent for a moment. We were both thinking the same thing. We both wanted to be back in our own homes, and in our own bodies, living our own lives.

But how?

Then I had a great idea. "The amusement arcade. Magic Mo!" Percy had put the money in and the machine had gone bananas.

"That must be it," Percy said. "We've got to go back there and do just what we did last time."

It had to work. I'd never prayed so hard. It just had to work.

Chapter 8
Game Over

There was the machine, humming softly in the back corner of the amusement arcade. Magic Mo. He looked helpful and kind with his smiling eyes. There was nothing odd about him.

The idea that it was a magic machine seemed crazy.

"We have to try," Percy said.

He felt scared like me.

"Put the money in," I told him.

He put the coins in the slot and we waited. For a minute or two nothing happened.

Then, all at once, Magic Mo came to life.
His eyes lit up. The lights flashed round his
head. Bells rang. The machine wailed and
moaned. Magic Mo seemed about to leap
from the screen.

I looked at Percy.

Nothing had changed.

This wasn't going to work. For one
awful moment I was sure it wasn't going to
work.

I closed my eyes and prayed. *Please.
Please. Let me be me again.*

I didn't open them until all the wailing
and moaning had stopped and Magic Mo
was humming softly once again.

The first thing I saw was my blazer.

MY blazer. No mess. No porridge. It HAD worked! I yelled at the top of my voice. "Percy! I'm me again!"

But Percy wasn't there.

He was waiting for me outside the arcade. He was sitting on the step with his head in his hands. His face was white. "Oh, Shawn. I was so scared."

I pulled him to his feet. "But it worked," I said. It was great to have my own voice back again.

"Do you know what I hated most about being you?" Percy said.

I began to laugh. "How could you hate anything about being me?"

"You couldn't tell a story to save your life," he said.

"That was the best thing about being you, Percy. You're great at telling stories."

We began walking along the road. "You are a good singer, you know," Percy told me. "I think you might end up a pop star or something. Maybe you could get into a boy band."

Now, I'd never thought of that. I wouldn't mind being a pop star.

"Of course," Percy went on, "you'd have to do something about that great big nose of yours."

Percy was laughing at me. I chased him down the street and grabbed hold of him. I put my hands round his neck as if I was going to strangle him. But we were both laughing. You'd think we were pals.

But I'll never be pals with Percy. No way! He might invite me to his home and the Baby from Hell might vomit all over me again.

But I'll never pick on him again. I know now Percy has enough to put up with.

We said goodbye. Percy was going home to his house, to his mother's awful cooking, his sisters who loved his stories and the baby who adored him.

I was going back to my Singing Mum!

As if he knew what I was thinking, Percy handed me a set of ear plugs.

"Here, use them," he said. "They really work."

I watched him walk away. He tripped over his laces again. This time I didn't laugh. Well, not a lot.

Percy turned back at the corner and waved. "By the way," he shouted, "you've got a date on Saturday night."

I smiled back at him. "Rebecca?"

He shook his head. "No, with Laura!"

Then he ran off. Laura, the ugliest girl in the school. Percy was a devil!

"I'll get you for that, Percy," I shouted after him.

In a way, I'd already got my own back. Just wait till he finds out about the ten mile hike I've put him down for at the weekend!

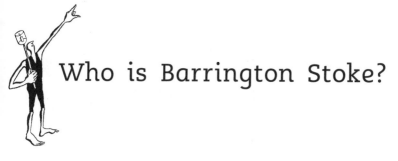

Who is Barrington Stoke?

Barrington Stoke went from place to place with his lamp in his hand. Everywhere he went, he told stories to children. Some were happy, some were sad, some were funny and some were scary.

The children always wanted more. When it got dark, they had to go home to bed. They went to look for Barrington Stoke the next day, but he had gone.

The children never forgot the stories. They told them to each other and to their children and their grandchildren. You see, good stories are magic and they can live for ever.

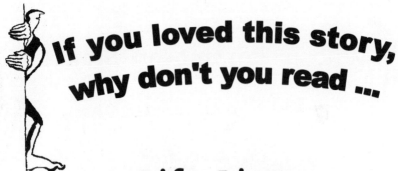

If you loved this story, why don't you read ...

Life Line

by Rosie Rushton

Have you ever told a fib because it was easier than the truth? Skid finds himself in trouble because he tells one fib too many. But how can he tell the truth about his home life?

4u2read.ok!

You can order this book directly from
our website: www.barringtonstoke.co.uk